Escape from Germany

Stories linking with the History
National Curriculum Key Stage 2

First published in 1998 by Franklin Watts
96 Leonard Street, London EC2A 4XD

Franklin Watts Australia
56 O'Riordan Street, Alexandria, Sydney, NSW 2015

This edition published 2002
Text © Penny McKinlay 1998

Editor: Kyla Barber
Designer: Jason Anscomb
Consultant: Dr Anne Millard, BA Hons, Dip Ed, PhD

A CIP catalogue record for this book
is available from the British Library.

ISBN 0 7496 4593 8 (pbk)

Dewey Classification 943.086

Printed in Great Britain

Escape from Germany

by Penny McKinlay
Illustrations by Greg Gormley

FRANKLIN WATTS
LONDON•SYDNEY

1

Berlin, 9th November 1938

CRASH!

The sound of shattering glass burst into Margot's dream. She sat up in bed. The curtains were rippling with red light from the street outside. She was scared, but she had to see what was happening.

She tiptoed to the window and looked out.
She gasped in horror. Across the road Herr
Lowenstein's shop was on fire. Flames
roared from the windows, leaping into
the darkness and falling back, like tigers
on a leash. Further down the street Heimpi's
sweet shop was ablaze.

Down below people were running, black
against the red firelight. Herr and Frau
Lowenstein were out in their
night-clothes, desperately
throwing buckets
of water at the
flames. But
worst of all
a crowd of
men stood
watching
and laughing,
throwing

stones at them
as people fought
to save their
homes. The
men wore
armbands
with bent
crosses on
them, swastikas,
and Margot
knew they were
Nazis, supporters of
Adolf Hitler, the German leader.

"You bullies!" Margot pounded her
fists on the glass. Someone looked up. She
realised with a shock it was Peter, the boy
from the next street who only last summer
had let her have a ride on his new bike. As
she looked down at him in horror, he bent
down to pick up a stone. She screamed as

he hurled it straight at her.

"Margot! Get away from the window, now!"

Papa pulled her away from the window just as the stone smashed through the glass, sending splinters all over the room. He held her close in his arms.

"Oh, Margot, you must not take such risks. They will hurt you!"

Margot was still furious, even though she was shaking with fear.

"But we must stand up to them, Papa! Look what they are doing!"

Papa pushed her away and held her
at arm's length, so she could see his face.
She realised only then that he was dressed
to go out, in
his overcoat.

"Margot,
listen to me."
Margot had
never heard
him sound so
serious. "The
Nazis are too
strong for us.
Sometimes all
we can do is find

a safe place and wait for
help. I want you to remember that. We
cannot stand up to them alone. We just
have to try and survive until the rest of
the world makes them stop treating Jewish

people like this. Now, listen very carefully," he said solemnly.

Mama had come in and was standing silently in the doorway. Five-year-old Max was clinging round her neck like a baby monkey, sobbing. They all jumped at the sound of banging on the front door. Papa went on: "The Nazis are taking all the men from this street away for questioning. You will have to be braver than you have ever been in your life before, Margot. You must help Mama, and look after Max, and maybe one day we will all be together again."

"Where will they take you, Papa?"

He hesitated. "To the police station, Margot."

"Not to the concentration camp?"

Margot wished she had not said those words as soon as they came out. They had all heard terrible things about what happened in the prison camps.

"I hope not," said Papa. The banging started again. "I must go, or they will take you too."

Papa hugged them all, and left them. Margot thought he was so brave, going off like that. They heard the tread of his feet on the stairs, step by step, and Margot wondered if she would ever hear that sound again.

Downstairs they heard him opening the door, rough voices barking orders, then heavy boots marching away down the street.

2
Night of Terror

That night seemed to go for ever. Shouts and screams in the street, smashing glass, crackling flames, falling timbers.

After Papa had gone they all climbed into Margot's bed together. They pulled the covers over their heads to block out

the noise and clung together to try to
stop shaking.

"When will Papa come home?"
asked Max.

"I don't know, Max," Mama replied.
"Soon perhaps."

Margot knew the truth. So many of
her friends' fathers had disappeared,
taken away by the Nazis. Some hadn't
ever come back. Anna's Papa had come
back, but he was like a different man,
so thin, so pale, so quiet. Anna said he
wasn't like her Papa any more.

They all jumped as something landed
on the bed. They thought
it was another
stone from
the street,
but it was
just
Gretchen,
Margot's
new ginger
kitten. She
was not allowed in bed.

"Please let her stay, Mama," pleaded
Margot. "She is so frightened." The kitten
was trembling.

"Just this once," said Mama. The
kitten settled down between them, under
the covers. Gradually she stopped shaking.

"Why are they doing this, Mama?"
Max whimpered.

"Because we are Jewish, Max,"
said Margot bitterly, before Mama could
answer. She was old enough to know the
answer, although she didn't understand.
"They hate us because we are Jewish."

Margot wondered how many times
she had asked the same question as Max –
why did all these bad things keep
happening to them? The answer was
always the same – "Because we are Jewish".

The worst day was when her friend
Elsbeth said she and her little brother

16

Gunther couldn't play with her and
Max any more.

"Mama says it
is forbidden,
Margot."
There
were tears
in Elsbeth's
eyes. "What
does it
matter, you
being Jewish,
anyway!" she cried.
"I don't care, you're my friend."

But that was the last time she ever
spoke to her. Next time they passed in
the street, Elsbeth's mother made her
children cross the road. Max cried but
Margot was angry. How could they hurt
little Max like that?

She remembered shouting at Mama: "I don't want to be Jewish any more!"

Her mother said: "You can't stop being Jewish, Margot. It's not like taking off a dress that doesn't suit you, or giving up dancing classes. It's what we are, what Omi and Opi are, and their Omi and Opi before them. We must be proud to be Jewish."

But it got harder and harder to be proud. So many things were forbidden to Jews – cinemas, theatres, even the wonderful Berlin zoo. Gradually more and more of their Jewish cousins and friends went to live in other countries.

"Why can't we go, Papa?" Margot had asked

"Because we don't know anyone who will promise to look after us, and without that, no country will take us." Papa always looked so pale and worried now.

Mama added quickly, "Papa is writing to lots of people, Margot. In the end someone will help us."

But nothing had been as bad as tonight. At last the terrifying sounds began to fade away, as their tormentors moved on to another Jewish street.

"They sound like a pack of wolves, Mama," said Margot.

"Yes, hatred has turned them into animals," replied Mama.

They were dozing into uneasy sleep when suddenly Margot remembered: "Heimpi's sweet shop, they set fire to Heimpi's sweet shop!"

Max sat bolt upright. "Mama, won't there be any more sweets?"

Mama laughed, a shaky sort of laugh that sounded so strange on such a night, and Margot and Max joined in. It was a relief but it felt very close to crying.

"Don't worry, Max," said Mama. "There will always be sweets."

3

"I Don't Like Bullies!"

Margot woke late the next morning. She
felt Max and the kitten in bed beside her,
and the memories of the night flooded
sickeningly back. Where was Mama?
Panicking, Margot raced downstairs.
She could hear voices in the living room,

and she burst in.

The room was full of boxes, and suitcases, with clothes and the best china and silver all strewn around the floor. Omi and Opi were there, and together they were helping Mama to pack everything.

"Where are we going, Mama?" asked Margot, frightened.

Max had came trailing into the room behind her and they both stood staring.

Margot had never seen Mama look like this before – her face red with crying, her hair loose instead of in a neat bun, wearing her dressing gown at breakfast time!

"We are going to live with Opi and Omi. We will be safer there, without Papa," said Mama. Max started to cry.

"It's all right, Max, everything will be all right," added Mama. "The most important thing is being together."

Omi came up and shooed them out.

"Margot, you must try and be a help, you're a big girl now," she said. "Take Max and ask the maid for your breakfast in the kitchen for once. Then you must take Max upstairs and keep him busy."

After breakfast Margot had to pull Max upstairs.

"I want Mama!" he wailed.

"No, Max, she's busy. But you can play with my treasures box if you're good."

She got him dressed and then left him playing happily with the box while she wandered over and looked out of the window. The tall houses opposite looked like a row of rotten teeth, every second or

third one burnt and black. Everywhere
their neighbours were sifting slowly
through their ruined homes, picking up
precious belongings. She turned away,
tears running down her cheeks. She loved
this house, how could she bear to leave it?

Gretchen was getting in the way,
trying to climb into the treasures box.
Margot picked her up and stroked her
while Max played with the bits of
jewellery, tickets saved from the
theatre, postcards from the zoo.

Everyone seemed so beaten and scared: Mama, Opi and Omi, the neighbours. But Margot didn't feel beaten, she felt angry.

Just then she noticed an old envelope Max had pulled out. Inside was a birthday card, with a message: 'To my little German daughter, who does not like bullies. With love, Lady Evelyn'.

Margot smiled. The card reminded her of when they first met Lady Evelyn Birch four years ago.

They were in the park with their nanny, Maria, when there was a sudden yelping behind them. It was a small spaniel, and it was cowering on the ground, being attacked by an Alsatian. It didn't stand a chance. Margot didn't stop to think. She seized a branch and ran at the dogs, waving it. The big dog lifted its head and stood growling at her, its teeth bared.

"Get off, get away!" shouted Margot and suddenly it turned tail and ran away.

"What a brave girl!" cried a woman's voice. Margot turned. There was the most glamorous woman she had ever seen – tall, with blonde waved hair, looking as if she had just stepped off a cinema screen.

"I don't like bullies," said Margot simply.

"Nor do I," said the lady. She was silent for a moment, staring at Margot as if she had seen a ghost. Then she introduced herself, in slow, careful German:

"I am Lady Evelyn Birch, I am English. My husband works here in Berlin. Can I come to your house to tell your parents how brave you are?"

And so they found a new friend. Lady Evelyn came to meet Mama and Papa and asked permission to take Margot and Max out for a treat. They went to the cinema and then to their favourite café right in the centre of Berlin for cream cakes and hot chocolate. That was back in the days when Jews were allowed treats like that.

The last time they saw Lady Evelyn was on Margot's eleventh birthday, and they went to her house in the wealthiest part of Berlin, and had proper English tea, with cakes called scones, and jam and cream. After tea Lady Evelyn hugged her.

"We're going back to England, Margot," she said. "We don't like what has happened to Germany since Hitler took over, especially what they are doing to Jewish people like you."

Margot noticed there were tears in her eyes. "You are so like my little girl, Margot. She was the same age as you when she died. Take care of yourself for my sake – and if you ever need help write to me." She pressed a tiny card with an English address written in gold into her hand. "Remember, I don't like bullies, either."

Of course! There inside the envelope was the little card still! She ran downstairs two at a time, clutching it.

"Mama!" she cried. "Lady Evelyn, she can help us escape

LADY EVELYN BIRCH.
GIBB HALL,
ROEGATE,
KENT.

to England! Then we will be safe!"

"Don't be silly, Margot," replied Mama, barely looking up from the boxes. She sounded so weary and hopeless. "She is not family, we hardly know her."

Opi said sharply, "Don't bother your mother now. We need to finish the packing."

Margot stomped back upstairs. They all seemed to be giving up.

She got out her best writing paper and started writing furiously to Lady Evelyn, almost stabbing the paper with her pen. It

all came pouring out, Papa being taken
away, everything being so awful. "Please
help us," she ended. "I know we are not
your family, but I know you are our
friend." She put Omi and Opi's address
and telephone number in the letter, so
Lady Evelyn would
know where
to find them.
Then she
copied the
English
address
carefully on to
the envelope, and
crept out to post it.

As soon as she stepped out into the
street she realised she had made a big
mistake. It wasn't like her street any more,
the friendly familiar place where she had

grown up, played hopscotch and skipped with her friends. It was terrifying. Everywhere she stepped there was broken glass from the shop windows. 'Jews Out' had been painted all over the doors, the stink of burning was everywhere.

All the way there and back she kept her eyes down, sick with fear in case she was stopped. She could hear passers-by laughing at what had happened to the Jews during the night. She boiled with anger inside, but she knew now what Papa had meant. She could not stand up to these people alone.

4
Waiting

Leaving home and moving in with Omi
and Opi was horrible. All their precious
belonging were parcelled up to be sold to
strangers. The children were only allowed
to take a suitcase of clothes and a few toys.
Everything else had to be sold. There was

no room at Omi and Opi's and, besides, they needed the money now Papa wasn't there to provide for them.

It was very boring, trapped inside all day, with only Gretchen to play with. Mama was scared to let them out to play in the street, and Margot had to entertain Max day after day through the cold grey winter weeks.

One afternoon Max was particularly restless.

"I'm bored!" he yelled, and threw the game across the room. "Why is everyone so cross? Why can't we have fun any more!"

Margot suddenly lost her

temper with him. "Because Papa has
gone away and is never coming back, you
stupid boy!" she shouted. Straight away
she wished she could un-say those words,
but it was too late. Max started to wail.

"I want Papa!"

Omi came in and picked him up.
Margot began to sob, the
first time she had cried
for weeks.

"I'm sorry, Omi,"
she cried.
"It's just everything
is so awful."

"I know, I know,"
Omi hugged her too.

"Listen," she said, when everyone
had stopped crying. "Let's have a waltzing
lesson, like we used to." And she put
one of her favourite old records on the

gramophone, from when she was a
young girl.

Then she swept them up in a waltz
around the room, round and round again.
At last they fell laughing and out of breath
in a heap on the sofa.

"Tell us about when you were a girl,
Omi," said Margot, and Omi told their
favourite old stories again, about all Omi's
boyfriends, and the dances she had gone
to and the dresses she had worn.

"That was in the old days, when
Berlin was a good place to be young,"
she said sadly.

Day after day passed and there was no
news of Papa. Opi made lots of telephone
calls, but no one could tell him where Papa
was, or when he would be released. The
grown-ups were always talking behind
closed doors, conversations that stopped as

soon as Margot or
Max came in.

One
day the
telephone
rang just
as Margot
was walking
past. She
answered it. It
was a crackling line,
and the voice was faint, but she knew at
once it was Lady Evelyn.

"Margot! Is that you? Thank God
you are safe, child!"

Lady Evelyn listened as Margot told
her everything.

Then she said: "Margot, I have
got permission for you and your family
to come to England but it may be more

difficult to help your Papa now he has been arrested. Now, go and get your Mama for me – you must leave Berlin quickly, before it is too late."

Margot brought Mama to the phone and hopped up and down beside her as she listened to Lady Evelyn. Mama looked puzzled, almost angry at first, then relief spread across her face. It was the first time Margot had seen her look happy for months.

At last, after a lot of talk about documents and arrangements, Mama put down the telephone and turned to Margot.

She caught her up and whirled her round the room.

"You've done it, Margot! We are going to live in England!"

5
Leaving Home

After that, everything was like a dream. Day after day the children went with Mama and queued up for hours in a gloomy office with hundreds of other silent, scared-looking Jewish people.

"Why do we have to wait, Mama?"

whined Max over and over again, and
Mama looked frightened in case the men
in uniform heard him.

She said: "Hush now, we have to get
our papers, Max. Don't make a fuss."

Like Mama, Margot was scared. She
had learned to fear the men in uniform
who ruled their lives. At the end of every
day, the man behind the desk barked: "Not
today, come back tomorrow!"

Margot thought of what Lady Evelyn had said: "Hurry. Leave Berlin quickly, before it is too late!"

But at last the day came when they got to the head of the queue and the man in uniform lifted his hand and stamped their papers. Once for Max, once for Margot, and once for Mama.

"But what about my husband – what will happen to him?" asked Mama.

"He is still under arrest," barked the man. "No decision has been made about him yet."

"But — " Mama was about to argue, but changed her mind. Her knees seemed suddenly to give way beneath her, and Margot had to help her to stand.

"Let's go, Margot," she whispered, and Margot helped her out of that terrible place, full of silent, frightened people.

That night as Margot lay in bed she could hear Mama arguing with Omi and Opi.

"I must wait until Karl gets permission to go with us. I can't go without him!" she was crying.

Then she heard Opi's deep, steady old voice.

"You must go, Lisl. It is the children who matter now. You must get them away to England where they will be safe from this madness. Perhaps he will be able to join you in England."

Then she heard Mama crying, and Margot cried too, silently in the darkness. How could they leave Papa behind? But she was so scared of staying.

On the morning they were due to leave, Margot knew without asking that she would not be allowed to take Gretchen. The kitten kept trying to climb into her satchel as she packed up her few things, as if she knew. Margot felt guilty about crying over leaving a kitten behind, when so many worse things were happening, but she couldn't stop the tears falling on to the kitten's thick fur.

At last Margot heard her mother calling. She went downstairs, Gretchen cuddled under one arm, her satchel swinging from the other shoulder.

There was a row of four suitcases in the hall, with everything they now possessed packed inside. One small one each for the children, one for Mama — and one for Papa.

Mama was still hoping desperately that somehow he would join them.

They struggled down to the car waiting outside to take them to the station. Margot looked back at the house one last time. Gretchen was at the front window, miaowing. Margot turned away quickly before she wept again, and got into the car.

When
they got to
the station
with Omi
and Opi,
they all
stood
around

awkwardly, not knowing what to do with
their last few moments together. Mama
looked about her anxiously, and Margot
knew she was still hoping that Papa would
suddenly appear.

The minutes ticked by on the big clock.

"You must get on the train now," Opi
said firmly at last.

Feeling sick, Margot climbed on with
Mama and Max. For the first time Max
realised that Omi and Opi weren't coming
with them.

"Why can't they come to England?" he wailed loudly.

"Hush!" scolded Mama, and he cried louder. She looked terrified at the noise he was making.

Margot leaned out of the train window, crying too.

"I can't leave you," she cried, stretching her hands out. "I love you so much."

"You must go, Margot," said Opi firmly. "You have your whole life ahead of you. We are old, Hitler cannot hurt us if you are safe."

"Now, Max, stop crying," said Omi gently.

"We have to stay – who would look after Gretchen?"

This seemed to calm Max, and he stopped crying, to Mama's great relief.

The guard was slamming the doors.

And then, at the last moment, Margot saw a man running along the platform. Too thin, too pale – but yes! It was Papa!

"Karl!" cried Mama. "Thank God!"

"Get on, my son!" said Opi. He and Omi held him for a moment, then pushed him through the door, just as the whistle blew.

"Goodbye!" they cried. "Goodbye!"

Margot watched her grandparents grow smaller as the train drew off, clutching each other for comfort. It was the last time she

would ever see them. Papa fell back on to the seat, gasping for breath.

Margot stared at him. It was like Anna had said, this pale, sick-looking man did not look like her Papa. He looked like an old, old man, and Margot felt frightened for a moment. Max slipped his hand into hers, as he stared too.

Then Mama hugged him close, and Papa stretched out his hands to the children and pulled them to him, and Margot knew it would be all right. They were one family again.

For those few moments Margot felt safe – almost – until there was a rap on the door and her heart sank at the sight of the familiar, hated uniform.

"Your tickets and papers!" the officer demanded. Mama pulled them from her bag. Her hands were shaking. Nobody dared breathe as he looked at their papers, then Papa's.

At last he snapped: "All in order!" and left.

It was the same every few hours throughout that long, anxious day. Mile after mile the train rattled on towards freedom and safety, but each time it stopped and their papers were checked it seemed their chance might be snatched away.

They hardly talked on the journey. Papa seemed content just to hold their hands, gazing silently out of the window as the fields and towns of Germany

flashed by. When Mama asked him
questions about prison, he shook his head.

"Not for the children to hear," he said
quietly. "I will tell you everything one day."

And then at last the border – the
last check of their papers – and the train
crossed into Holland.

They were free.

It was evening when they stepped off
the train and smelt the sea air of the Dutch

port. Before them was the ship that would
take them to England. They stood on deck
watching as the crew untied the ship's
ropes. Darkness fell on the land as they left
it behind them.

"Have we escaped? Are we free now?" asked Max.

"Yes," said Papa.

"A strange thing to say about home," said Mama bitterly.

"It is not our home any more," said Papa. "Germany did not want us and we are no longer Germans. England will be our home now."

And they turned and looked out across the grey sea towards their new country.

Refugees

This story about Margot and her family is made-up, but it is the sort of thing that happened to many Jewish families who became 'refugees' from Germany before and during the war.

A refugee is someone who is forced to escape from their own country because they are being badly treated or might be killed there, or have lost their homes through war. They have to find a home in another country.

The Jews

Jewish people are descended from peoples who lived in Israel many centuries ago. The Jews spread all over the world, but sometimes the local people did not like them, and feared them because they seemed 'different' from themselves. This is what we call 'racism', when people treat other people badly or differently because of the colour of their skin or their beliefs.

Adolf Hitler

Six years before the war between Britain and Germany began, in 1933, a man called Adolf Hitler became the leader of Germany. He led a political party called the Nazis. At that time many people in Europe did not have jobs and were very poor. Adolf Hitler hated the Jews and he told the German people that they were taking their jobs and money away.

He passed many laws that made life difficult for Jewish people. They could not have well-paid jobs, like doctors or lawyers. They had to wear a yellow star badge to show they were different. Jewish children could not go to the same schools as other German children and were even forbidden to play with them.

Those Left Behind

Many thousands of Jews left Germany. However they could not go to unless someone in the country they went to would promise to pay for them. The ones who did escape were the lucky ones, starting new lives in new countries, like Britain and America. Many Jewish children went on their own, without even their parents.

Many thousands of Jews were left behind, like Margot's grandparents. They, like the Jews in all the countries the Germans occupied, were treated with appalling cruelty.

Many millions of people, including babies, children, their parents and grandparents, were taken to concentration camps and were killed there. These tragic events have become known as the 'Holocaust'.

When people in other countries found out what

was happening to the Jewish people they wanted even more to defeat Germany to stop this cruelty.

Sparks: Historical Adventures

ANCIENT GREECE
The Great Horse of Troy – The Trojan War
0 7496 3369 7 (hbk)   0 7496 3538 X (pbk)
The Winner's Wreath – Ancient Greek Olympics
0 7496 3368 9 (hbk)   0 7496 3555 X (pbk)

INVADERS AND SETTLERS
Boudicca Strikes Back – The Romans in Britain
0 7496 3366 2 (hbk)   0 7496 3546 0 (pbk)
Viking Raiders – A Norse Attack
0 7496 3089 2 (hbk)   0 7496 3457 X (pbk)
Erik's New Home – A Viking Town
0 7496 3367 0 (hbk)   0 7496 3552 5 (pbk)
TALES OF THE ROWDY ROMANS
The Great Necklace Hunt
0 7496 2221 0 (hbk)   0 7496 2628 3 (pbk)
The Lost Legionary
0 7496 2222 9 (hbk)   0 7496 2629 1 (pbk)
The Guard Dog Geese
0 7496 2331 4 (hbk)   0 7496 2630 5 (pbk)
A Runaway Donkey
0 7496 2332 2 (hbk)   0 7496 2631 3 (pbk)

TUDORS AND STUARTS
Captain Drake's Orders – The Armada
0 7496 2556 2 (hbk)   0 7496 3538 X (pbk)
London's Burning – The Great Fire of London
0 7496 2557 0 (hbk)   0 7496 3122 8 (pbk)
Mystery at the Globe – Shakespeare's Theatre
0 7496 3096 5 (hbk)   0 7496 3449 9 (pbk)
Plague! – A Tudor Epidemic
0 7496 3365 4 (hbk)   0 7496 3556 8 (pbk)
Stranger in the Glen – Rob Roy
0 7496 2586 4 (hbk)   0 7496 3123 6 (pbk)
A Dream of Danger – The Massacre of Glencoe
0 7496 2587 2 (hbk)   0 7496 3124 4 (pbk)
A Queen's Promise – Mary Queen of Scots
0 7496 2589 9 (hbk)   0 7496 3125 2 (pbk)
Over the Sea to Skye – Bonnie Prince Charlie
0 7496 2588 0 (hbk)   0 7496 3126 0 (pbk)
TALES OF A TUDOR TEARAWAY
A Pig Called Henry
0 7496 2204 4 (hbk)   0 7496 2625 9 (pbk)
A Horse Called Deathblow
0 7496 2205 9 (hbk)   0 7496 2624 0 (pbk)
Dancing for Captain Drake
0 7496 2234 2 (hbk)   0 7496 2626 7 (pbk)
Birthdays are a Serious Business
0 7496 2235 0 (hbk)   0 7496 2627 5 (pbk)

VICTORIAN ERA
The Runaway Slave – The British Slave Trade
0 7496 3093 0 (hbk)   0 7496 3456 1 (pbk)
The Sewer Sleuth – Victorian Cholera
0 7496 2590 2 (hbk)   0 7496 3128 7 (pbk)
Convict! – Criminals Sent to Australia
0 7496 2591 0 (hbk)   0 7496 3129 5 (pbk)
An Indian Adventure – Victorian India
0 7496 3090 6 (hbk)   0 7496 3451 0 (pbk)
Farewell to Ireland – Emigration to America
0 7496 3094 9 (hbk)   0 7496 3448 0 (pbk)

The Great Hunger – Famine in Ireland
0 7496 3095 7 (hbk)   0 7496 3447 2 (pbk)
Fire Down the Pit – A Welsh Mining Disaster
0 7496 3091 4 (hbk)   0 7496 3450 2 (pbk)
Tunnel Rescue – The Great Western Railway
0 7496 3353 0 (hbk)   0 7496 3537 1 (pbk)
Kidnap on the Canal – Victorian Waterways
0 7496 3352 2 (hbk)   0 7496 3540 1 (pbk)
Dr. Barnardo's Boys – Victorian Charity
0 7496 3358 1 (hbk)   0 7496 3541 X (pbk)
The Iron Ship – Brunel's Great Britain
0 7496 3355 7 (hbk)   0 7496 3543 6 (pbk)
Bodies for Sale – Victorian Tomb-Robbers
0 7496 3364 6 (hbk)   0 7496 3539 8 (pbk)
Penny Post Boy – The Victorian Postal Service
0 7496 3362 X (hbk)   0 7496 3544 4 (pbk)
The Canal Diggers – The Manchester Ship Canal
0 7496 3356 5 (hbk)   0 7496 3545 2 (pbk)
The Tay Bridge Tragedy – A Victorian Disaster
0 7496 3354 9 (hbk)   0 7496 3547 9 (pbk)
Stop, Thief! – The Victorian Police
0 7496 3359 X (hbk)   0 7496 3548 7 (pbk)
A School – for Girls! – Victorian Schools
0 7496 3360 3 (hbk)   0 7496 3549 5 (pbk)
Chimney Charlie – Victorian Chimney Sweeps
0 7496 3351 4 (hbk)   0 7496 3551 7 (pbk)
Down the Drain – Victorian Sewers
0 7496 3357 3 (hbk)   0 7496 3550 9 (pbk)
The Ideal Home – A Victorian New Town
0 7496 3361 1 (hbk)   0 7496 3553 3 (pbk)
Stage Struck – Victorian Music Hall
0 7496 3363 8 (hbk)   0 7496 3554 1 (pbk)
TRAVELS OF A YOUNG VICTORIAN
The Golden Key
0 7496 2360 8 (hbk)   0 7496 2632 1 (pbk)
Poppy's Big Push
0 7496 2361 6 (hbk)   0 7496 2633 X (pbk)
Poppy's Secret
0 7496 2374 8 (hbk)   0 7496 2634 8 (pbk)
The Lost Treasure
0 7496 2375 6 (hbk)   0 7496 2635 6 (pbk)

20th-CENTURY HISTORY
Fight for the Vote – The Suffragettes
0 7496 3092 2 (hbk)   0 7496 3452 9 (pbk)
The Road to London – The Jarrow March
0 7496 2609 7 (hbk)   0 7496 3132 5 (pbk)
The Sandbag Secret – The Blitz
0 7496 2608 9 (hbk)   0 7496 3133 3 (pbk)
Sid's War – Evacuation
0 7496 3209 7 (hbk)   0 7496 3445 6 (pbk)
D-Day! – Wartime Adventure
0 7496 3208 9 (hbk)   0 7496 3446 4 (pbk)
The Prisoner – A Prisoner of War
0 7496 3212 7 (hbk)   0 7496 3455 3 (pbk)
Escape from Germany – Wartime Refugees
0 7496 3211 9 (hbk)   0 7496 3454 5 (pbk)
Flying Bombs – Wartime Bomb Disposal
0 7496 3210 0 (hbk)   0 7496 3453 7 (pbk)
12,000 Miles From Home – Sent to Australia
0 7496 3370 0 (hbk)   0 7496 3542 8 (pbk)